14 Days

NOV 17, 1980   JUN. 22 1983   JUN. 2 0 1981
MAY 13 '81   JUN. 2 4 1983   JAN 1 3 1992
JUN 2 '81   AUG. 29 1983   FEB 1 4 1992
JUN 29 '81   SEP. 1 9 1983   DEC 1 6 1993
[JUL 6 '81]   OCT. 2 6 1983   [DEC 1 7 1994
JUL 14 '81   NOV. 1 9 1983   [JAN 3 1 1995
SEP 23 '81   JAN. 4 1984   FEB 1 4 1995
OCT 7 '81   SEP 2 8 1995
[OCT 23 '81]   JAN. 3 1 1984   [JUL 3 1996
FEB 4 '82   MAY 2 5 1984   JAN 1 6 1997
APR 1 '82   MAY 3 1 1984   JUL 1 2 1997
APR 2 '82   JUN. 9 1984   FEB 1 9 1998
               JUN. 2 1 1984   FEB 4 2000
APR 23 '82   JUL. 1 0 1984   JAN 2 '08
MAY 5 '82
JUN 8 '82   AUG. 6 1984
SEP 20 '82   SEP. 1 2 1984
OCT 4 '82   JAN. 7 1985
NOV 8 '82   APR. 8 1985
               AUG. 3 1 1987
APR. 1 5 1983 MAY 2 7 1988
JUN. 1 1 1983 JUN. 2 2 1988

WITHDRAWN

Harold Thinks Big

by Jim Murphy
Illustrated by Susanna Natti

Esther is a breathtaking cheer-leader. Smitten with her tiny black toes and the way she yells "Sooma-lacka, sooma-lacka," Harold de-cides he must win her love. Think BIG! says his lawyer, so Harold devises a very Big Plan.

It includes:

> a green flag
> a flashing scoreboard
> a blimp
> a love song
> and *hundreds* of balloons.

Does the plan work? Not perfectly, or even the way it's expected to. But thinking BIG!, as Harold realizes, is sometimes not the only way to go. . . .

Harold Thinks Big

by Jim Murphy
illustrated by Susanna Natti

Crown Publishers, Inc. / New York

For Elaine Kelso (alias Mom-Catz)

Also by Jim Murphy
Weird & Wacky Inventions

The text of this book was set in 16 point Plantin. The illustrations were prepared as black halftone drawings with separations, prepared by the artist, for red and yellow.

Library of Congress Cataloging in Publication Data   Murphy, Jim, 1947–   Harold thinks big.
Summary: Harold devises an elaborate scheme to try to get Esther to notice him.
[1. Pigs—Fiction]   I. Natti, Susanna.   II. Title.   PZ7.M9535Har   [E]
79-24199   ISBN 0-517-53912-8

Contents

Love at First Sight

One day Harold was playing
on the monkey bars
with Willy and Susie.
"I'm hungry," he said.
"Let's get some french fries."
They left the park
and walked by the football field.
The Poonton Bay Porkers
were practicing.

"Who's that?" asked Harold.
"That's Esther," Willy said.

6

"She's the cheerleader
for the Porkers."

Harold looked at Esther
for a long time.
He loved her curly hair
and her tiny black toes.
And he loved the way
she yelled,
"Sooma-lacka! Sooma-lacka!
Hit'm in the head!
Push'm back, Porkers.
Kill'm dead!"

"I wish she would yell
sooma-lacka, sooma-lacka for me,"
said Harold.
"Esther already has a boyfriend,"
said Susie. "His name is Bruiser."
"And he's bigger than a tree,"
said Willy.
"I don't care," said Harold.

"I want Esther to notice *me*."

"Send her candy,"
  Willy said.

"Candy always gets my attention."

"Tell her you like her,"
  said Susie.

"I have a better idea,"
  said Harold. "Wait here!"

He ran home and picked
the biggest pumpkin
in his garden.

Then he washed it
and carried it back
to the football field.

He walked right past
Susie and Willy and
headed straight for Esther.

"My name is Harold," he said.

"And this is for you."

"Oh, Harold," said Esther.

"How sweet of you."

"Sweet!" said Bruiser.

"Did you hear that, fellas?
   This guy is SWEET!"

Bruiser picked up the
pumpkin and kicked it.
It sailed into the air
and broke into
a thousand pieces.

"It didn't even bounce,"
    said Bruiser.

"Now Bruiser," said Esther.

"Be nice."

"Okay," said Bruiser.

"Let's play some football, Harold."

"I don't know," said Harold.

"I'm not very good at sports."

"Don't worry," said Bruiser.

"I'll teach you."

The Game

Harold followed Bruiser
onto the football field.
"Put this helmet on,
    and hold the football
    under your arm."
"Then what?" Harold asked.

Bruiser walked to
the 50-yard line.
"Then try to run past me
to the goal line."

"Be careful, Harold!"
shouted Susie.
Esther yelled,
"Sooma-lacka! Sooma-lacka!
Run, Harold. Run!"
Willy covered his eyes.

Harold puffed up his chest
and made a mean face.
He put his head down
and ran as fast as
his little legs
could carry him.

When he had almost
reached Bruiser,
he turned to the right
and tried to run
around him.
But Bruiser jumped
on top of him.

"Oooofff!" said Harold.
"Did you say something?"
asked Bruiser.

"Yes," said Harold.
"Get off me."

"Want to try again?"
  asked Bruiser.
"No," Harold said.
"Don't feel bad," said Esther.
"At least you tried.
  I admire a pig who tries."

Willy helped Harold
stand up.
Susie brushed grass off his jacket.
"See you soon, Harold,"
 Esther said.
"Yeah," said Bruiser.
"See you real soon."

"I think Esther likes Bruiser
better than you," said Susie.
"But she said she admired me,"
said Harold. "And she said
she would see me soon."
"She was only being polite,"
said Willy.

"Some friends you are,"
  said Harold.
"We're only trying to help,"
  said Susie.
"Your kind of help
  I can do without," said Harold.
"So long!"

Harold went home
and sat
in his favorite chair.
He tried to think of a way
to win Esther's heart.
But he kept hearing
Esther's voice:
"Sooma-lacka. Sooma-lacka.
I love Harold lots."
He went into the kitchen
and made a cup of tea.

As he squeezed lemon into it,
he thought of Owl.
"Owl is a lawyer,"
thought Harold.
"And lawyers
know everything."

The Big Plan

Harold sat in a wooden chair
in Owl's office
and told him all about Esther.
He told him about her curly hair,
her sooma-lacka cheers,
and the nice things
she had said to him.

He also told Owl about Bruiser.
Owl leaned back in his chair
and lit a cigar.
"You came to the right owl,"
he said.
"I knew I could count on you,"
said Harold.
"Tell me what to do."
Owl blew a smoke ring
that landed on Harold's nose.

"First, you must learn
   to believe in yourself."
"What else?" asked Harold.
"You've got to think big,"
   said Owl.
"Big?" asked Harold.
"Yes," said Owl. "BIG.
   Do something BIG for Esther
   and she'll come running to you."

"That's it!" said Harold.

"I've been thinking too small.

From now on,

I will think BIG!"

Harold walked to the door.

"How can I ever thank you?"

"Don't worry," said Owl.

"I'll send you a bill."

Harold walked through the forest.
Soon he thought of a plan.
The plan became
bigger and bigger.
He hurried home
and made fifteen phone calls.
"Esther is sure to love my
BIG Plan," he thought.
"And she is sure to love me too."

Harold and Esther Forever

On Saturday Harold went
to the football game.
He sat in the very first row.
Bruiser tackled
every runner who came near him.
He picked up a fumble,
kicked a field goal,
and caught three passes.
But Harold did not care.

At the end of the game
Esther yelled,
"Sooma-lacka! Sooma-lacka!
Bruiser passed the test.
Bruiser scored all the points.
Bruiser is the best!"
Harold stood on his seat.
He took a green flag
out of his pocket
and waved it.

The scoreboard lit up.

It said:

The band played a love song
and made giant letters
that spelled:
Harold and Esther.

Harold climbed over the fence
and ran across the field
waving his flag.
A blimp sailed over the field

and hundreds of balloons
fell on the ground.
Each one said:
Harold and Esther Forever.

Esther ran toward Harold.
Her cheeks were bright red.
"Are you crazy?" she shouted.
"I love you!" said Harold.
"Love!" said Esther.
"You don't even know me.
You must be out of your mind."
She took Harold's flag
and broke it in half.

Bruiser tapped Harold on the shoulder.
"If you go near Esther again,
I'll kick you into another state."

Harold stood in the middle
of the field
all by himself.
Balloons bounced everywhere.
"This isn't what
I had planned on," he thought.
The band played the love song
as Harold walked off the field.

No More BIG Plans

Harold went to the park
and sat on a rock.
"No more BIG Plans," he said.
"BIG Plans are stupid!"

"No, they're not," said Susie.
"What are you doing here?"
   asked Harold.
"I thought you could use
   a little company," said Susie.
"You don't think I was dumb?"
   asked Harold.
"No," said Susie.
"Or silly? Or pigheaded?"
"No, and no again," said Susie.
"In fact, I thought it was fun."

"Well, Esther didn't think so."

"Esther doesn't know what fun is."

"Did you like the balloons?"
   asked Harold.

"I loved the balloons," said Susie.

"Balloons are the only things
   that are rounder than I am."

"I know where there's a field
   full of them," said Harold.

"Then let's go!" shouted Susie.
And they ran through the park
and all the way back
to the football field.